Weekly Reader Children's Book Club presents

The Magical Drawings

# of Moony B. Finch

David McPhail

DOUBLEDAY AND COMPANY, INC.   GARDEN CITY, NEW YORK

Copyright © 1978 by David McPhail
All Rights Reserved
Printed in the United States of America

ISBN: 0-385-12103-2 Trade
       0-385-12104-0 Prebound

Library of Congress Catalog Card Number 76-23778

McPhail, David M.
    The magical drawings of Moony B. Finch.

    SUMMARY: Talented artist Moony B. Finch discovers
that his drawings can come to life.
    [1. Magic—Fiction] I. Title.
PZ7.M2427Ma   [E]

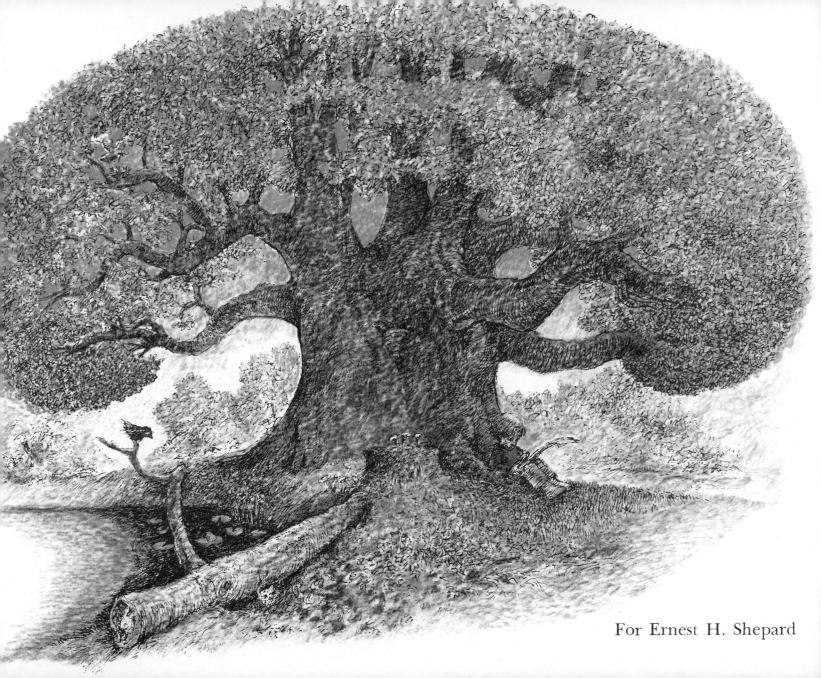

For Ernest H. Shepard

Moony B. Finch loved to draw.

For his second birthday he was given a box of crayons.
After that, he spent most of his time drawing pictures.

He drew

and drew

and the more he drew
the better he got.

Moony would draw pictures even when he didn't have any paper.
In the summer, at the beach, he drew pictures in the sand with a stick.

And in the winter, he drew giant pictures in the snow with his feet.

He drew things inside

and he drew things outside.

He drew things he saw

and he drew things he imagined.

Moony had an eraser that he called his *just-in-case* eraser.

He never used it, but he always carried it with him
just in case he ever needed it.

One day at the park, Moony was drawing
a picture of a cloud.

"What a marvelous drawing," said a lady
who just happened to be passing by.

"May I have it?"

Moony handed the lady the drawing and when she touched it, the cloud lifted right off the paper and floated down the path.

"Wait!" cried the lady, as she went running after it.

"That was amazing!" said the man sitting next to Moony on the park bench. "How did you do it?"

"I don't know," replied Moony. "Nothing like this has ever happened before."

"Will you draw something just for me?"
asked the man. "Like a pirate's treasure chest
filled with gold coins?"

"That's easy!" said Moony,
and with a few quick strokes
of his crayon it was done.

The man picked up the drawing and when he did,
the treasure chest slid off the paper
and landed in his lap!

Gold coins spilled out of the chest and rolled down
the sidewalk, attracting a large crowd.

A woman with a baby came pushing through the crowd.

"How about a picture of a diamond-studded silver rattle?"
said the woman to Moony. "For my baby."

Moony had hardly finished the drawing when the woman
grabbed it right out of his hands!

Instantly, the rattle fell off the paper and tumbled
into the carriage with the baby.

Then a bearded old man stepped forward.

   "Sonny," he began.
   "Moony," corrected Moony.
   "Whatever," said the old man. "I get so tired hobbling
around on my gimpy leg, I'd feel much better if I had a
picture of a chauffeur-driven limousine to look at.
If you please, for an old man."

The request was quickly granted. When the old man touched the paper,
the limousine slid off and rolled over his toes.

Everyone in the crowd began pushing and shoving and yelling
at Moony, "Draw this for me! Draw that!"

Moony stood up on the bench and shouted as loud as he could,
"Please be quiet!"

When the crowd hushed, Moony continued. "Hold still!" he said.
"I want to draw a picture of everybody!"

Ties were straightened, hair combed, and make-up freshened
as Moony tore three pieces of paper from his drawing pad.

On the first piece, he drew a picture of the smiling crowd—
the man with his treasure chest, the woman, her baby, and the silver rattle,
the old man and his limousine, and all the people
who wanted Moony to draw them a picture.

When the drawing was finished, Moony took his
just-in-case eraser from his pocket.
Taking pains to be neat, Moony erased
the treasure chest with all of its gold coins,
the silver rattle, and finally the chauffeur-driven limousine.
    And as Moony erased them from the drawing, they
disappeared from the clutches of their greedy owners.

The crowd murmured,
then buzzed, then charged angrily right at Moony.
Taking his second piece of paper, Moony drew
the fiercest dragon that he could imagine.

When Moony tossed the drawing into the crowd,
everyone scrambled to get it!

The instant someone touched the paper . . .

the dragon sprang to life, roaring and breathing fire!
All the people ran for their lives!

Even the bearded old man was gone in a flash!

With the crowd gone, the dragon turned on Moony.

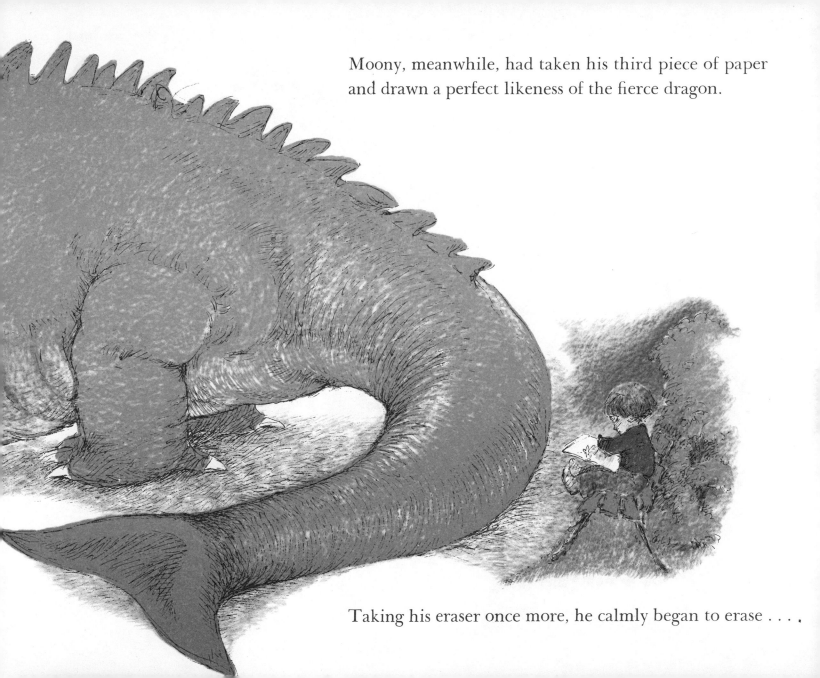

Moony, meanwhile, had taken his third piece of paper
and drawn a perfect likeness of the fierce dragon.

Taking his eraser once more, he calmly began to erase . . . .

the terrible teeth . . .

the razor-sharp claws . . .

the powerful tail.

And when the drawing was entirely erased,
the dragon disappeared!

For a long while Moony sat on the bench, thinking.
With great care he drew one last little picture.

Then he put his *just-in-case* eraser back in his pocket,
and with his drawing pad under his arm, he headed for home.